2003 11 04

For my children
forever,
no matter what

First published in Great Britain in 1999
by Bloomsbury Publishing Plc
First U.S. edition 1999

Library of Congress Cataloging-in-Publication Data
Gliori, Debi.
No matter what/Debi Gliori.
p.   cm.
Summary: Small, a little fox, seeks reassurance that
Large will always provide love, no matter what.
[1. Parent and child—Fiction.   2. Love—Fiction.   3. Foxes—Fiction.
4. Stories in rhyme.]   I. Title.
PZ8.3.G47No   1999
[E]—dc21   98-47277
ISBN 0-15-202061-6

J K I

Printed in Hong Kong

The illustrations in this book were executed in watercolor
and ink on 100 percent rag, acid-free watercolor paper.
The display type was set in Artcraft.
The text type was set in Bernhard Modern.
Printed by South China Printing Company, Ltd., Hong Kong
U.S. edition designed by Lydia D'moch

No Matter What

Debi Gliori

Harcourt, Inc.

San Diego   New York   London

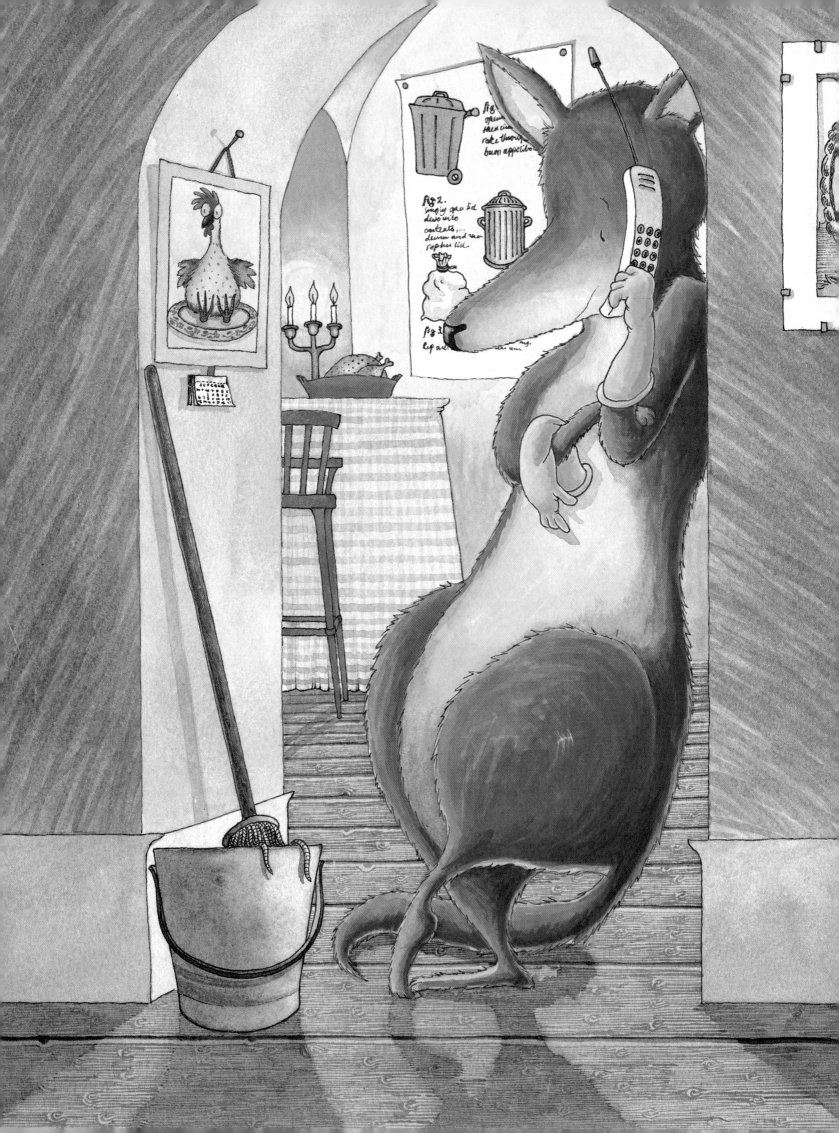

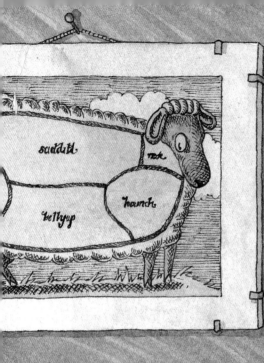

Small was feeling
grim and grumpy.

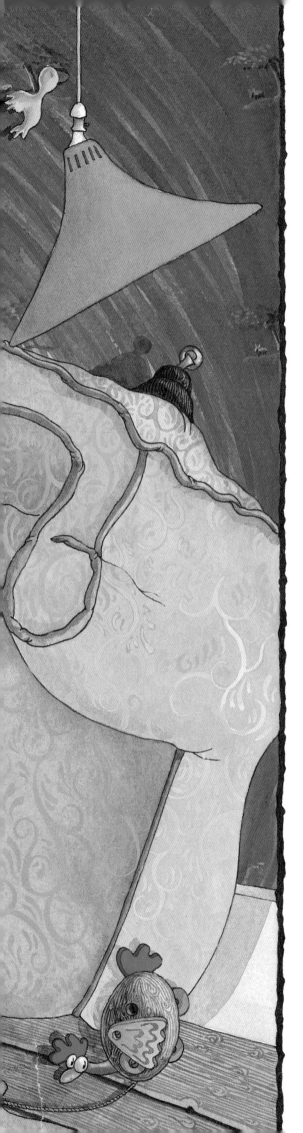

"Good grief," said Large.
"What *is* the matter?"

"I'm grim and grumpy,"
said little Small,
"and I don't think
you love me at all."

"Oh, Small," said Large,
"grumpy or not,
I'll always love you,
no matter what."

"If I were a grumpy grizzly bear,
would you still love me?
Would you still care?"

"Of course," said Large.
"Bear or not,
I'd always love you,
no matter what."

"But if I turned into a squishy bug,

would you still love me and give me a hug?"

"Of course," said Large.
"Bug or not,

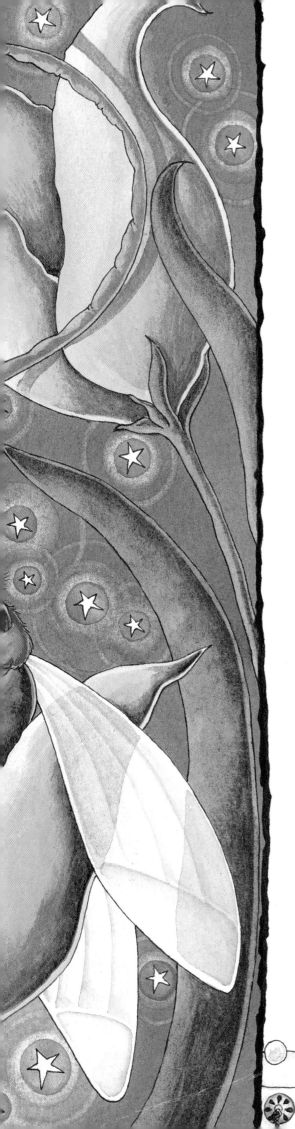

I'd always love you,
no matter what."

"No matter *what*?"
said Small with a smile.

"I'd still hold you close and snug and tight,
and tuck you up in bed each night."

"But does love wear out?
Does it break or bend?
Can you fix it or patch it?
Does it mend?"

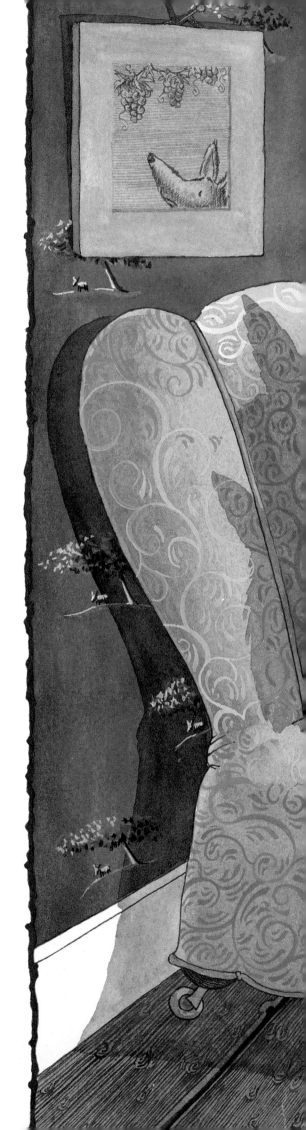

"With time together, a smile, and a kiss—
love can be mended with things like this."

"But what about when you're far away?
Does your love go too, or does it stay?"

"Look up at the stars.
They're far, far away.
But their light reaches us
at the end of each day."

"It's like that with love—
we may be close, we may be far,
but our love still surrounds us . . .
wherever we are."